Peace Is Not a Seamless Web

By
Joel M. Allred

For information address:
Joel M. Allred, 416 Maryfield Drive,
Salt Lake City, Utah 84108
Email: joelmallred@msn.com

Image and Photo Credits: *See page 213.*

ISBN 978-0-9773955-2-1

Library of Congress Control Number: 2007907472

FIRST EDITION

Contents

Every spirit builds itself a house; and beyond its house a world; and beyond its world, a heaven. Know then that the world exists for you. For you is the phenomenon perfect. .... All that Adam had, all that Caesar could, you have and can do. Adam called his house, heaven and earth. Caesar called his house Rome; you perhaps call yours, a cobbler's trade; or a scholar's garret. Yet line for line and point for point, your dominion is as great as theirs though without fine names. Build, therefore, your own world.

Ralph Waldo Emerson

Prologue

PROLOGUE

* * *

He was first noticed as a sturdy youth tending fertile fields in a tranquil place where the law of the harvest governed.

He was next remembered as a soldier in a terrible war in a turbulent place where the law of the harvest had been repealed –

Evil men reaped where they had not sown.

He was a brave soldier who cheated death in trying times on distant fields.

Though he rarely spoke of the war, it seldom left his mind.

He returned to the land of his fathers a thoughtful, seasoned, decorated man.

prologue

The boy who first tended fertile fields then fiercely fought in war became the Teacher.

* * *

He spoke of freedom and truth.

"Freedom is sacred," he said.

"Freedom is more important than wealth or peace."

"Freedom is more important than comfort, security, celebrity, acceptance or friendship."

"Truth is more important than power."

"Truth has warts, needs no softening and has but a single face."

"Truth is more important than comfort, security, celebrity, acceptance or friendship."

He cautioned them.

> *[L]et the counsel of thine own heart stand:*
>
> *For there is none more faithful unto thee than it.*

For a man's mind is sometime wont to bring him tidings,

More than seven watchmen, that sit above in a high tower.

Ecclesiastes

* * *

He listened more than he spoke.

But when he spoke, this is what he said:

Examine your lives.

Go where you have not gone.

Discover what doesn't meet the eye.

Draw conclusions after first considering facts.

Always take a second look.

Never fail to further inquire.

Follow your intellect where it leads.

And he said this:

It is sometimes said that the voice of the people is the voice of God.

prologue

A dissenting voice is not evidence of impiety.

Freedom bellows when silence is sweet.

Freedom has roots in rebellion.

Liberty is not a lap dog.

Discipline governs appetite.

Preach and practice restraint.

And he said this:

No one owns the truth.

Managed truth is not inspired.

Tyranny homesteads in closed minds.

Certainty is mother to many mistakes.

Tyranny is tidy.

Freedom is chaotic.

Absolute power corrupts.

And then he said:

Doubt is not wicked.

In the marketplace of ideas, no settlement is ever final.

Science succeeds because it is first tentative and skeptical.

Be quick to admit you were poorly informed.

Feel blessed to find you are better informed.

Trust yourself and deny your genius nothing.

* * *

So did he speak.

Some took offense.

Others listened and learned.

He did not encourage disciples,

But there were those who faithfully followed him.

When they left, he remembered them.

Where they went, they remembered him.

In this way, the Teacher's legend spread.

He said this to them:

Facts are stubborn things.

Faith is not the victory of feelings over facts.

No one should ever be punished for telling the truth.

If you are not first free, whatever else you are is not enough.

* * *

His once bright flame was flickering now.

His hair was white, and his face was lined and weathered.

Tremors caused his hands to shake, and his gait was unmistakably awkward.

Time had taken its toll.

Although he listened intently, his words were slow.

Now they summoned him.

"Teacher," they said, "lend us your lips."

"Tell us," they said, "what you have learned."

"Say what you have not already said."

"Instruct us one more time."

"Let those who love you inquire."

When he saw them gathered, he was touched.

But when he rose to counsel them, the Teacher's voice was strong.

Enlightenments

ESSENTIALS

"What is Essential?" they first inquired.

Effort.

Sacrifice.

Judgment.

The wise use of time.

Have you glorified what is trivial?

Have you neglected what is not?

Have you spoken empty words?

Must you be first?

Do not tilt at every windmill, hoping to win the lottery with luck and little effort.

Do not think to say that when things are different you will do this or that.

When things are different, you will be the same.

Who doesn't have an agenda?

Customers, clients, constituencies –

Miles to go, bills to pay, mouths to feed?

Do everything, but do what is important first.

Promote cherished values.

Find needs and fill them.

Set goals and reach them.

ISTENING

"Why do you Listen?"

Those who speak compete for your respect.

Those who listen gain your trust.

Respect is an acquaintance.

Trust is a friend.

Trust is greater than respect.

Guard secrets like a priest.

Find the power in restraint.

Let those who trust you feel secure.

listening

He was warming to his task.

CERTAINTY

"Why quarrel with Certainty?"

How would you be valued?

By your acts, or by your truth?

Does your heart condemn you?

Are you cursed by your doubt or blessed by your virtue?

Are you threatened by your temptation or redeemed by your restraint?

When you understand something imperfectly, say that you do.

When the ground beneath your feet begins to shake, say that it does.

certainty

If you are wrong, admit it.

If you don't know, don't say that you do.

If you are not certain, don't say that you are.

Certainty is death to the open mind.

The truth is never complete.

There is much you will never know.

There are mysteries you will never solve.

Certainty denies the need to further inquire.

ETERMINING TRUTH

"What is true, how do we know and what does it mean to us?"

There are no unassailable propositions.

The inquiring mind finds peace in probabilities.

The "t" in "truth" is written lower case.

May your critical faculties resist seduction.

May your principles meet the test of common sense.

Let propositions present credentials.

Draw conclusions after first considering facts.

Seek to understand before you presume to explain.

Dare to disobey.

Treat with contempt those who sell their vision with threats,

For those who trade in threats are friends of order and enemies of truth.

There are many voices of truth.

Seek them out and learn from them.

Consider what is new.

Reconsider what is not.

Never leave the thinking to others.

Value truth.

Say what you mean.

Let those offended rage.

Whatever you are,

Whatever you think,

Whatever you know,

And however you feel –

Live an exemplary life.

COURAGE

"Who are the objects of our bounty? How shall we defend them?"

Necessity is the mother of courage.

Desperation makes you strong.

But does it make you brave or wise?

If you are backed against a wall by evil men,

And your loved ones are behind that wall,

Will you defend them?

Who would not?

courage

But will you interrupt a brutal beating by a monstrous assailant to save a stranger?

Will you stick your nose deep into someone's violent altercation?

If it is good to defend loved ones instinctively,

It is better to defend strangers by choice.

Have you spoken against injustice?

Have you faced down threats?

Have you protected those who couldn't protect themselves?

Have you considered the needs of distant siblings?

Humanity is the object of your bounty.

Courage stiffens in tempests.

Never say yes to retreat.

Stand when others sit.

CONSCIENCE

"What of limits and choice?"

You are a law.

Conscience is the law of the inner life.

If the Master provides the sketch, you furnish the detail.

If the Master determines the floor, you determine the ceiling.

With plans come choices.

Conscience is the clearing house for choice.

Conscience is discretion's court of last resort.

Conscience manages complexity.

Conscience imposes order upon chaos.

Conscience deploys deeply hidden resources.

Put space between yourself and temptation.

Let no one demand what conscience can't provide.

Sweet are the uses of restraint.

Do no harm.

Never cheat.

Avoid mistakes.

Treat everyone fairly.

Respect the law of your life.

LAW

"Speak of the Law."

When the will of the sovereign is law,

When law is but whim and happenstance,

Hawks eat pigeons when they find them.

Where there is no law, there is no freedom.

Where there is no freedom, there is no justice.

When freedom and fairness fail, Goliath rules.

The law is the pilot light of democracy.

It is the task of the law to establish boundaries,

To maintain order, resolve disputes, restrain abuse and transfer power peaceably.

Ordinary civilians control powerful armies because of the law.

Contentious cultures live together in peace.

Men and women are equal.

Those accused have rights.

The law rewards cooperation.

It encourages enterprise, protects the injured, and holds offenders to account.

It is the law that substitutes dialogue for killing fields.

What crowds do in violence, courts do in peace.

/NALIENABLE RIGHTS

"Do hawks eat pigeons in heaven?"

Suppose that:

You are the architect,

The master of planning,

The director of protocol,

The guardian of every virtue,

And the father of every family.

Suppose that:

You are the draftsman drawing the plan,

The engineer making the calculations,

The developer of every project,

The foreman of every crew,

And the master of detail.

Suppose:

You are the mayor,

The chief of police,

The district attorney,

And the presiding judge.

What will you make of your domain?

How will you build and rule?

Will you be patient?

Will you bridle your anger and exercise restraint?

Will you reward ingenuity and forgive mistakes,

Encourage discretion and tolerate complaints?

Will you be kind to your critics?

Suppose:

That you are in charge of curriculum,

That you evaluate and hire the personnel,

And determine who sits on the governing board.

What will you make of your power?

Will you promote ruthless bondage?

Will you charter secret police?

Lay down tyrannical rules?

Will you encourage respect for law?

Will the opinions of others count?

Will the governed give consent?

Will power be limited?

And exercised respectfully?

Will rules be subject to interpretation?

Will there be due process?

Equal protection and rights to respect?

Will you encourage virtue or demand nothing less?

Will you promote justice, or will you rule in shame?

Will you be followed, right or wrong?

Will what you say be the end of every discussion?

Shall anyone do as they please?

Time will tell.

GO

"Is Ego a virtue?"

Ego is tolerable – but in a tiny dose.

While the subtle scent of fine perfume is provocative,

The same scent applied in excess may turn passion to disgust.

A compulsive ego is smallpox without a vaccine.

It is swagger out of control and a tax on enterprise.

Ego denies what ego demands.

Anxious for respect, it invites contempt –

Because flawed motives discourage respect.

Humility is ego's antidote.

Free from tasteless exaggeration,

Immune to trifling considerations of importance or rank,

Humility requires little recognition and has no need of praise.

Ego exalts self over service, turning everything inward.

Humility cedes the stage to others.

Ego is conceit.

Humility is not.

Ego complicates.

Humility simplifies.

Ego spreads contention.

Humility promises peace.

Exaggerated egos cheapen good works.

Selfish intentions make wholesome objectives suspect.

How wretched is shameless ego –

How long on self importance and short on cooperation.

How more sincere is silence.

How more virtuous is understatement.

How more honorable unpretentious sacrifice.

How sweet is ego tamed.

CIVILITY

"Is Civility dead?" It was a politician who said.

You disrespect dissent.

You promise the world.

You communicate in anger.

You despise competing visions and speak over them.

You treat the marketplace of ideas like a war zone,

And you insist on being front and center.

Surprised but not contrite, the man did not retreat.

"Leaders oughtn't bend in every wind."

"We are up to our necks in alligators."

Then drain the swamp.

But do not fix your feet in bronze.

Measure your inflated pride against your stunted flexibility.

Be slow to anger and quick to forgive.

Promote polite and civil discourse.

Seek clarity and consensus.

Espouse the greater good.

And compromise.

Do not whip with your displeasure those who disagree with you.

TERROR AND TRUTH

"Who speaks for truth when terror calls the tune?"

Honesty is the goddess of virtues.

Credibility is her reward.

Reputation follows those who speak the truth.

Would you be well remembered?

Always speak the truth.

When fear is contagious,

When terror is center stage,

When deception threatens truth,

When honesty is the exception and something else the rule,

Dissidents are heroes, and defiance is virtue.

When freedom is suppressed and truth is ignored,

Intrepid souls emerge from unpredictable places to nourish the human spirit.

The pillars of the temple are honesty and truth.

Would you live to see the temple in ruins?

Would you start the demolition?

Disrespect the truth.

Heroes weigh command against conscience.

Heroes speak the truth to swaggering power.

So do they separate themselves from crowds.

ARRIAGE AND TRUST

"What of Marriage? And what of Trust?"

Marriage is the cornerstone,

The start of the beginning,

The key to contentment.

Is your home a place of peace and repose?

Do you share your secrets and tell each other the truth?

Are you soul mates?

Do you live for each other?

Do you hold nothing back?

Do you give whatever you have?

Loyalty is the beginning and end of relationships.

Loyalty is the glue that holds everything else together.

It is the pledge you make to those who place their trust in you.

Will you ignore your commitment?

Will you set at naught your sacred pledge?

Will you inflict misery on those who love you?

Discipline is the enemy of appetite.

Loyalty is the wall temptation cannot climb.

Love and commitment are delicate values.

Like sunflowers sprouting in shade, they require nurturing care.

Fidelity is about example – integrity, trust and honor.

It is about protecting investment and growing eternal together.

Values predict results.

Avoid decisions made in haste.

Never put those you love at risk.

Those who cheat those they love will cheat anyone.

Those who disappoint their children will disappoint strangers.

Don't make mistakes you must explain to your children,

Or think to teach them to be principled if you are not.

Children directed by dependable parents more often than not arrive secure.

Home, marriage, children, fidelity and faith.

Would you have peace?

Embrace!

COMING TOGETHER

"How shall we Come Together?"

Jesus was not a terrorist, and heaven is not a rogue state.

Jesus trafficked with sinners and publicans.

He forgave seventy-times-seven.

He treated those who made mistakes with great respect.

He was woman at the well go-thy-way and sin-no-more sensitive to frailty.

Dare to abandon your circle of privilege.

Allow your understanding to conquer your fear.

Commingle.

Respect diversity.

Practice inclusion.

That which others esteem may mean little or nothing to you.

That which you esteem may mean little or nothing to them.

Exclusion is simple.

Understanding is complex.

Those who would divide you say, "We know what is best for you, and it isn't fraternity."

Those who would unite you say, "We will love you and live with you in peace."

Avoid the rhetoric of polarization.

Unite.

Do not divide.

Humanity is the object of your bounty.

Respect what means everything to others.

ALUES

"How shall neglected Values be reclaimed?"

How shall goodness fare when pagan self assertion trumps Christian self denial and impulse rules?

When the social order surrenders to depravity, unprincipled children become unprincipled adults.

Without strong values, adults set poor examples and children misbehave.

When evil claims a seat at the head of the table,

Pity those who dutifully challenge corruption.

Who will bravely start the next great revival?

Who will describe forgotten truths to this generation?

Who will inspire today's disciples to leave everything and follow?

When those who are evil overwhelm those who are not,

When genius leaves the temple and haunts the market,

When culture is deception,

When truth is ignored,

And leaders are flawed,

Step up, speak out, be heard.

Risk your comfort.

Shout defiance.

HEPHERDS

"What of Shepherds?" he said. "So many say they speak for God. How shall we know them, follow them and live?"

What do those shepherds say?

"He has told us what is good for you," they say.

"You speak in local terms to your own small flock."

"He tells you what they need to know, and you tell them."

"We speak in global terms to everyone."

"He tells us what everyone needs to know, and we tell you."

"When we have spoken," they say, "the thinking has been done."

"Accept our words and govern yourselves."

"Reject our words and live at risk."

"Make your peace with us and with Him who tells us everything you need to know."

"Follow us or the author of evil; claim the peace of the blessed, or live forever in sin."

"These are words of warning; we are gods to you."

But what if He has not told them what is good for you?

What if He doesn't tell them everything everyone needs to know?

What if what they say He says is only what they say?

What if He has told them nothing?

What if they don't speak for everyone and are not global thinkers?

What if their domain is not as great as yours?

There are those bold to say:

"We only of all have seen the light and know the way."

"We own the words of life; put your trust in us; we can not mislead you."

There are those bold to say:

"We speak to God; God speaks to us."

"Whatever God requires is right, no matter what it is."

What is true?

Pious fraud is pious fraud.

Spiritual chains chafe and bind.

Authoritarian rule is authoritarian rule.

Indoctrinated children become compliant adults.

What is true?

Tyrants command and coerce, as they traffic in absolutes.

Leaders struggle with uncertainty in a less than perfect world.

Distinguish leadership from tyranny.

Distinguish leaders from tyrants.

Embrace leaders; reject tyrants.

Refuse to be coerced.

Dare to disobey.

Ignore authoritative teaching.

Let no one tend your store.

Follow truth wherever it leads.

Thoughtful disciples think for themselves.

Who deserves immortality?

Those who reject authoritarian keepers.

Avoid invisible fetters.

Avoid freedom-defeating entanglements.

Trust yourself and deny your genius nothing.

Reject pretentious shepherds.

Turn everything foolish away.

Do not shade, neglect, conceal, ignore or turn from truth.

Speak without meddlesome intermediaries to Him who sent you here.

Virtue does not belong to the brazen few.

RIENDSHIP

"Friendship?"

Know who you are.

Never lose sight of yourself.

Do not mistake trappings for reality.

As you strive to become the person you want to be,

Never forget the person you actually are.

Play the cards that you were dealt.

Make strangers friends.

Draw them out and see them as they are.

And if you would know their secrets, aim low.

To explore someone's secret soul,

To visit someone's sacred place,

Is an extraordinary privilege.

Opportunities knock.

Fleeting chances come and go.

Friends communicate on fields of secrets.

They shed their earthly trappings,

And share their precious trust.

No one will ever know you until you let them.

Open closed doors.

Put yourself at risk.

Let others do the same.

Like what you see of yourself.

Respect what others let you see of them.

Friends see through smoke.

FAITH, FEELINGS, FACTS

"Speak of Faith. What of Faith, what of Feelings, what of Facts?"

Is there a faith-promoting reality begging to be shared?

Is there a faith-disturbing reality that needs to be suppressed?

Thoughtful disciples refuse to distinguish public from private reality.

Things should always be seen as they are.

The facts of faith should never be suppressed.

Those who lie for the Lord are deceivers.

Those who ignore and conceal the truth are deceivers.

No honorable disciple perpetuates error,

Seeks to mislead unsuspecting believers to salvation,

Or attempts to defend what doesn't deserve a defense.

Truth has warts, needs no softening and has but a single face.

If the truth is confusing, it is confusing.

If the truth is disturbing, it must speak for itself.

What isn't faith promoting isn't faith promoting.

Truth is bold.

Those who speak it are brave.

Those who ignore it are not.

Does the Lord look with favor upon those who mold facts to their liking?

Does He counsel with those invested in secrecy?

With censors and deceivers and apologists?

When leaders misrepresent, select, exclude, ignore, suppress, conceal, neglect, forget, confuse, distort or torture truth,

The great message of life becomes "a tale told by an idiot, full of sound and fury signifying nothing."

History is an institution's resume.

History is a measure of deportment.

It describes what is past and predicts what is future.

Scratch-the-surface disciples build shallow lives around unsupportable facts.

Faith demands intelligent inquiry and honest disclosure.

There are those who function in a cloistered world,

Calling each other "president this" or "president that,"

Who are never called to account.

Sequestered disciples ignore contradictions,

And accept momentum as evidence of truth.

Does the Spirit ignore deceit?

Encourage misrepresentation?

Favor things determined false?

Is faith the victory of feelings over stubborn facts?

What is less than the truth is never enough.

PASSION

"Passion rules the waves. But is it love?" The *skeptical father winked.*

The Teacher knew the student well.

Who introduced you to passion?

Who minted the magic seed that called your children forth?

What distant acts of creation inspired life's yearning for itself in you?

Have you thought this miracle through?

Do you know the Great Biologist?

Have you given thanks?

Are your children accidental?

Do you deny the existence of a creator when you are one?

What price have you paid for the power to hurl your image through eternity?

In your fertile loins lie insistent forces demanding and finding expression, as God makes His great work your own.

Before he was the father of civilizations, Abraham was smaller than a dot.

The patriarch's boundless posterity was at first a tiny message board.

Are you too a patriarch?

Do you honor to your longing?

Is the promise of your posterity boundless?

Are you destined to become the father of civilizations?

If all the world is a stage with Passion but a player, consider the script with care.

Aspire to divinity – partner in the wonders of creation, lest you be fallen, tormented and incomplete.

LOVE

"Love is more than genetics."   So did the gentle mother speak.

Love is for parents, children and siblings,

For family, neighbors and friends –

No one is out.

True love is not a combustible.

Love is a peaceable force in a thoughtful place.

It is less tumultuous but more complicated than passion.

Who shall feel pain at judgment?

Feudal masters, false prophets, tycoons, tyrants, torturers and thieves,

Pedophiles, perjurers, murderers, rapists and burglars.

Dictators, deceivers and demagogues –

All those who have not loved.

And who shall be at peace?

Dedicated teachers, brave thinkers, dependable parents,

Enlightened employers, thoughtful disciples,

Poets, peacemakers, principled leaders,

Those invested in freedom and truth,

And generous volunteers –

All those who have loved.

For love is legal tender there.

Love is a peaceable force in a thoughtful place.

*H*EROES

"How are Heroes measured?"   A man of peace inquired.

Have you deserving heroes?

Would not pacifists also be heroes?

Have you exemplars of passion and firm resolve?

And then he related this:

On the day after the festival of the Holy Innocents, shortly after Christmas in the year 1170, Archbishop Thomas Becket was murdered in the Canterbury Cathedral upon orders from King Henry II.

When the King's unruly knights confronted and cursed the lamb in the Cathedral, he "coloured deeply, . . . seeing . . . they had come for his hurt." After he replied to their disrespect, they countered and said that he had spoken in peril of his head.

"Do you come to kill me?" he then inquired. For, "I have committed my cause to the Judge of all; wherefore I am not moved by threats, nor are your swords more ready to strike than is my soul for martyrdom."

After the knights insisted he flee the kingdom, he firmly said, "*. . . no one shall see the sea between me and my church. I came not to fly; here he who wants me shall find me.*" The Archbishop's words, uttered in defiance of his earthly King, were quickly followed by the knights' brutality.

Will your goblins "see the sea" between yourself and your place of peace?

Will terrifying assassins find you on the path of duty bravely waiting martyrdom?

Will you hold fast your station and reject the urge to fly?

Are you prepared to do what fortune may require of you?

Heroes step up when cowards step down.

They challenge arbitrary authority and encourage change.

Heroes are soldiers in trenches, nurses in intensive care, princes of the church and bespectacled scholars.

Heroes languish in jail, preach disobedience, console the unwashed, lead great movements and visit the moon.

Heroes unlock the secrets of life, defeat disease, care for the demented, sacrifice for humanity and teach their children well.

ARTYRS

"Is decency endangered? Is punishment certain and swift? Are martyrs avenged?"

The Teacher paused before answering:

The assassin stood briefly on the railing before leaping awkwardly from the slain leader's box to the stage of the theater.

The heel of his boot caught in the ornamental bunting that marked the distinguished victim's special place, causing the man to land on one knee and break his leg. The symbol had taken revenge.

The man quickly stood, despite the injured leg, as if to say, "I am not hurt."

But the scene was something less than the accomplished actor might have hoped –

it would be a poorly executed if temporary humiliation.

Now fashionably dressed in black, with raven hair and flashing eyes,

Handsome to a fault, resolute and somehow strangely calm,

The assassin recovered his poise.

As he walked behind the footlights,

He turned to the audience and said,

"Sic semper tyrannis."

When words rehearsed were finally spoken,

Sparing terms carefully chosen to explain a terrible act,

The actor limped from the stage, mounted a rented horse and disappeared.

In the disturbed mind of the swarthy assassin there lived a hero,

A tormented patriot whose memory would surely be blessed by the passage of time.

"A tree is best measured," the victim's biographer said, "when it is down."

This particular fallen oak was quickly measured immortal.

And the grim assailant?

The assassin who murdered the saint?

The man with raven hair and flashing eyes?

That disappointed soul languishes in infamy,

By his disappointed mother's side in an unmarked grave.

History has long since judged his last performance harshly.

"Sic semper tyrannis" – "Thus always to tyrants."

VIL

"Have you seen the face of Evil?"

The Teacher sadly answered, "Often."

When liberators entered the death camp after conquering brutal guards, they found one million suits and dresses, great mounds of spectacles, dentures and shoes, and seven tons of human hair.

Hatred has a life of its own.

People angry about this may take revenge on that.

They forget the cause of their anger as they attend to the object of their present rage.

Demagogues,

Masters of misdirection,

evil

Saddle rage and ride.

Evil is general.

Humans are specific.

Hatred is no respecter of persons.

Generalized hatred affects specific humans indiscriminately.

Is it in you? Even a bit?

Victims are ciphers to predators –

Things without weight, worth or influence –

Inconsequential objects of no importance.

What does it matter that you kill a child?

For what is today a maggot is tomorrow a fly.

Starve those humans to death.

Freeze them to death.

Beat them to death.

Suffocate them.

March them to death.

Work them to death.

Let them die of disease.

Rape them.

Torture them.

Hang them up.

Shoot them in large pits.

Gas them in secret chambers.

Burn them in gigantic ovens.

What shall ever be said of such monstrous evil?

What possessed them to commit outrageous murder on such a massive scale?

Were these monsters mutants sprouted from some black lagoon?

Indestructible perennials destined to surface again some time soon?

Will evil ever be extinguished? Probably not.

Will it always challenge the brightest hopes of humanity? Probably so.

Is it in you?

Are you like them?

Could you do what they did?

EADERSHIP

"How shall we Lead?"

Leaders are complicated.

Some are larger than life; others are easy to ignore.

Some are naturally skilled; others are elaborately trained.

Issues make leaders.

Issues more important than leaders make leaders more important than themselves.

For those who lead, the time is always now.

The world is alive with possibilities.

Leaders traffic in possibilities.

Leaders, lend us your ears.

Be thoughtful if you fail;

Accept the blame.

Be gracious if you succeed;

Share the credit.

Great leaders cast long shadows.

MANAGED TRUTH

"Is Managed Truth inspired?"

The unexamined life is wasted and unworthy.

Belligerent disciples trivialize scholarship and lack respect for truth.

Are these Dobermans destined for divinity?

Shall mine-is-but-to-do-or-die disciples gain the prize?

Is God so shallow?

Is He at war with republican principles?

Is He the infallible author of an authoritarian plan?

Does He demand unthinking obedience and live in fear of the facts?

Does He frown upon freedom of expression and thought?

Does His rage outweigh His humanity?

Is God dogmatic?

Do heretics threaten Him?

Will dissenters be punished with fire?

Shall the wicked burn as stubble on the great and terrible day?

Is mindless certainty the only acceptable reaction to doubt?

Must the faithful always impose preexisting conclusions upon new and unsettling facts?

Does flattery pleasure Him?

Does He favor disciples who bear false witness?

Does He hold in high esteem those who suppress and conceal the truth?

Are censors called and chosen?

Is God the sponsor of secret vaults and censorship?

Do good and faithful servants know but fail to teach the truth?

Do disciples who shield the flock from facts find favor with Him?

Are they defenders of the faith and heroes?

Or charlatans and frauds?

Is God appalled when thoughtful disciples have conflicting visions?

Does He love uniformity and despise dissent?

Does God manage truth?

And approve the efforts of those who do?

Shall the uninformed inherit the kingdom of heaven?

Do apologists find favor with Him?

Does the demand for truth exceed the supply?

Must history be sanitized, reworked to seem polite?

Managed truth is not inspired.

Thoughtful disciples discover and tell the truth.

Incorrigibles find purpose and meaning in faith-promoting error.

The facts of faith should never be suppressed.

No one should ever be punished for telling the truth.

TEWARDSHIP

"When shall the lion lie down with the lamb?"

What were those battlefields but dreadful places where ideas were tested by trial –

Slavery, sovereignty, freedom and the rule of law?

Stewards are society's dependable sentries.

They let nothing bravely won be lost.

Some comfort-obsessed stewards violate sacred trusts.

Pampered hedonists, strangers to discipline –

They surrender the kingdom for calm.

There are contentious shepherds, divisive figures who betray the flock,

Citizens who despise their sacred heritage, but stand for nothing themselves.

Every generation must pass the torch –

From those who created a great legacy, who sacrificed and thought of others first,

To those determined to protect that great legacy, who sacrifice and think of others first.

Safeguard your sacred inheritance.

When duty calls, stalwart stewards stand their stations – whatever the cost.

Are you prepared to protect your values?

Every value every time?

When shall the lion lie down with the lamb?

When shall swords become plowshares?

Brave stewards will tell.

CHILDREN

"How shall the Children grow?"

You are creators;

You are artists and curators;

Role models, guardians and mentors.

Remember this:

The growing season is short.

Be good shepherds; tend your flocks with care.

A child is not a small adult.

Recall as a parent how you felt as a child.

Teach values.

Give your children space.

Provide opportunity.

Encourage good habits.

Promote high standards.

Praise everything of good report and offer incentives.

Share their joy.

Feel their pain.

Treat them with great respect.

Have them help; show them how.

Draw your saber as a last resort.

Never betray a child.

Children who distrust adults are destined to resemble them.

Teach them in small steps slowly.

Write with honor on small clean slates.

"And what if nothing works?" The familiar voice implied defeat.

Did you teach them everything you could?

Or did you expose them to your example and leave their lessons to chance?

Did you direct them to a seemingly safe harbor?

Or did you provide challenging options and invite choice?

Did you demand humility?

Did you demand obedience?

Are they humble?

Or do they misbehave?

Are their boundaries poorly defined?

Are they comfortable with confusion, or better off coerced?

Teach freedom.

Recognize courage.

And reward initiative.

You are the gardener.

You till the soil, plant the seeds and nurture them.

Till the soil, plant the seeds, tend the garden, step aside and let the flowers grow.

ARENTS

"What do children owe parents?"

Parents invest.

Worthy children are the return.

Society assigns the sins of children to parents.

But what if parents have not reaped as they have sown?

What should be said to parents whose harvest is shame?

To those who have seen small returns on big investments?

When strong parents beget weak children, "nothing grows in the shade."

When neglectful parents beget neglectful children, "the apple falls close to the tree."

But when responsible parents beget irresponsible children, "something doesn't meet the eye."

Children are not created equal.

Successful children are not an entitlement.

Discipline is a tight wire.

Parents ought walk that wire with caution when the weather is calm.

Too little may spoil the child.

Too much may encourage rebellion.

What do children owe parents?

Respect, good will, loyalty and gratitude.

Parents take justifiable pride in children with integrity.

What is suitable payment for a devoted parent's intangibles?

Principled children living useful lives.

Children who demonize parents sometimes fail themselves.

Children:

Respect advice.

Forgive and forget.

Treat parents like the people you wish they were.

Children in ascendancy?

Gently pass parents in decline.

ICTORY AND DEFEAT

"What if we Fail?"

Shall anyone escape the "slings and arrows of outrageous fortune"?

The stripes that mold and stiffen resolve?

Those destined to succeed must first determine to finish well,

Willing to venture, hoping to gain, seldom distracted,

Win, lose, better, worse –

Always consistent,

Never deterred.

In life, results are close.

Victory is a narrow thing.

One vote may decide an election.

A single straw may break a camel's back.

Success may be measured in hundredths of seconds.

Do not gloat if you succeed,

Do not whimper if you fail.

Avoid arrogance and reject despair.

Good times pass; hard times intervene.

Victory is fleeting, and defeat is not forever.

AIRNESS

"What is Fair? And what if Fairness fails?"

At its best,

Fairness is instinct –

Instant, unconsidered,

Like a dependable reflex.

It is an element of conscience.

Do genocidal monsters busy cleansing the earth,

Do brutal masters of mind control,

Consider good and evil?

Practice fair?

Feel pain?

Fairness is the prick against which evil kicks.

It is the uncomfortable burr on a tyrant's saddle.

Does it begin with you?

Are you fair?

Will you cheat to get something you don't deserve?

Will you claim the credit for someone else's work?

Will you take what doesn't belong to you?

Do you bend the rules?

Do you stretch the truth?

Do you feed at the bottom of the pond?

If citizens carry their grievances into the streets, if crowds do in violence what courts do in peace,

If dissenters are neutered with drugs,

If women can't vote or go to school,

If Jews wear yellow stars,

And books are burned,

Fight to the death.

DVERSITY

The woman, terribly thin and eerily pale, said only this: "Adversity?"

Adversity is an unwelcome guest.

And when she calls, she overstays.

What shall be said for suffering?

You give something up –

You get something back.

You pray for strength –

What you get are problems.

Solving problems makes you strong.

Suffering shaped the gods.

Peace is ever inconstant.

Hard times pass.

Those consumed by relentless adversity must adapt.

If life on earth is a spit in the bucket,

If mortality is but a single scene in one of a thousand acts of a great eternal play,

See it through.

Stay the course.

Never admit defeat.

REEDOM

A single mother, a toddler at her side, wondered about "Freedom."

The answer, although softly spoken, was confrontational.

Your choices are impulsive and poorly considered.

Your appetites lead to consequences not of your choosing.

You have heard that freedom is a "shining city on a hill."

Now hear this: "The road to the landmark is checkered with potholes."

Freedom is like a large buffet, where diners decide every day what to eat.

Some will fill their plates with healthy choices.

Others will eat and drink to wretched excess.

Freedom is a terrible curse to the poorly behaved.

You must draw your line in the sand before the battle begins.

Only a fool would think to cross the Rubicon without a plan.

Where there is liberty, there is choice.

Where there is liberty, there is license.

In a place that celebrates one and tolerates the other,

Some will brightly shine; others will predictably stumble.

Who has not heard this: "I am free and will do as I please"?

Freedom is more than the right to do as you please.

It is not the absence of boundaries.

You have heard that "mother's choice trumps baby's pain."

You have heard that "a fetus is not really a person."

Are these foundations of freedom?

Is murder ever a choice?

If a woman has the right to marry a woman because that is her preference,

If a man has the right to marry a man because that is his preference,

If the institution of marriage is to be more finely tuned,

Why can't a woman marry a man and a woman?

Or half a dozen women, or half a dozen men?

Why can't a man marry a woman and a man?

Or any number of either or both?

And if a man can marry a man,

And a woman can marry a woman,

And if convention is to be more finely tuned,

Why can't an adult cohabit with a consenting child?

A man with a boy?

A woman with a girl?

A man with a girl?

A woman with a boy?

Or a brother with a sister,

If that is their preference?

Or a lawyer with a client?

Or a doctor with a patient?

Or a teacher with a student?

Or a priest with a parishioner?

Not everything on display in that large buffet is easy to digest.

Reckless choices lead careless persons in awkward directions to absurd results.

Is freedom the absence of rules?

Is it the utter abandonment of common sense?

Is whatever anyone wants the definition of freedom?

Is each man's personal preference every man's constitutional right?

Discipline is freedom's friend.

Freedom has boundaries.

Society sets them.

Freedom is a state of bliss reserved for those who preach and practice restraint.

ECADENCE

"Give me peace at any price! Is there a hidden cost?"

Decadence is cancer moving in stealth to raging disease.

It is the wasting of the spirit.

It is the embrace of excess.

It is peace at any price –

Appeasement.

Decadence lives for the moment.

It is bribes and shameful concessions;

It is corruption and humiliating compromise;

Weakness in the face of strength;

Bargains with devils;

Tolerance for evil.

Decadence is a short-term plan for decaying cultures and a stage in the decline of freedom.

It pays lip service to virtue in the pursuit of power.

Decadence is bad judgment looking for the line of least resistance.

It is low people with low tastes thinking low thoughts, setting poor examples and offending decency.

Decadence is a whistle stop – the station where depravity catches its breath on what is a long day's journey into night.

When sin is a habit,

Flawed leaders lead,

Stewards violate sacred trusts,

Parents scribble on clean slates,

And soldiers abandon their posts.

Tempests rage, and no one cares.

Decadence is soiled culture.

Its churches are empty,

Its parents are corrupt,

Children misbehave,

And no one cares.

Decadence defends the murder of innocent infants,

As it opposes the execution of culpable adults.

Nothing of value is worth a defense.

The world is upside down.

Indifference is virtue.

decadence

Good is evil.

Faith is cold.

God is dead.

ELF GOVERNANCE

"How shall we live to our Light?"

The easily distracted man had been on different sides of many issues.

Are you a soldier in someone else's army?

Are you a satellite in someone else's orbit?

Are you some stronger person's lengthened vocal cord?

A muffled voice with never an independent thought?

Take charge.

Think strong.

Tend your store.

Treat your conscience with respect.

Keep faith with yourself and others.

Celebrate eccentricity and never rush to judgment.

Work without direction.

Bring insight to every task.

Avoid freedom-defeating entanglements.

Forswear talking points and surrogacy.

Tolerate less than perfect order.

Respect freedom of choice.

Stay out of debt.

Freedom is not a lap dog.

Independence is annoying.

One man's glory is another man's threat.

Freedom has roots in rebellion.

Freedom bellows when silence is sweet.

Blessed are they who live to their values and govern themselves.

RESPECT

"When shall we enjoy Respect?" An unmarried
black father inquired.

Your values leave much to be desired.

Your entertainment is carnal and corrupts your
youth.

Your children are born out of wedlock.

You are poorly educated and slow to change.

You commit terrible crimes and lack respect for
law.

Demagogues pander to your dependency.

You are stuck in reverse and your needs are never
met.

respect

"How shall we be redeemed?" **The soft reply took the Teacher by surprise.**

Revisit marriage.

Read to your children.

Send them to school,

And follow them there.

Close the quarrel with the past.

Choose well-intentioned leaders.

Avoid welfare and respect the law.

Turn on those who promote sex and violence in your music and culture.

Cultivate virtue.

Appreciate beauty.

Treat women with respect.

Set a good example.

Look forward to the future.

Seek everything of good report.

Reclaim your family.

Stand for something good.

Preach and practice self control.

And remember this: *Respect is always earned.*

PTIMISM

"Is Optimism justified?"

Who can be sure?

And why should it matter?

For what is more essential?

Optimism is the language of life.

It is the centerpiece of every master plan.

Optimism explored the frontier and colonized.

Every soaring vision,

Every lovely flight of fancy,

Every enviable accomplishment,

Begins and ends there.

It is the indispensable ingredient in every savory mix.

Optimism makes everything work.

Optimism makes everything better.

Optimism built whatever was built – everything that ever was.

$\mathcal{P}$ROCRASTINATION

"My congregation Procrastinates. What would you say to them?"

Procrastination precludes achievement a day at a time.

It doesn't say something can't be done, inviting firm resolve.

It says, "Not today," "There is plenty of time," or "Sometime soon."

Procrastination is the place of repose for under-achievers.

Procrastination prevents failure by delaying choice.

Not to try, it says, is not to fail.

Set what is shallow aside.

Tell your congregation this:

Narrow your focus to whatever is first.

Discipline bids you live with no regrets.

That to which you aspire is more important than what you have today.

Seek to secure timeless values.

Take orderly aim at distant goals.

"By the inch, it's a cinch; by the yard, it is hard."

Emphasize everything plain and precious.

Concentrate on cherished objectives.

Do everything important now.

INDUSTRY

"What makes for a happy shop? Speak of Industry."

How are plans completed and great needs met?

How is nature tamed and the law enforced?

Through effort and industry.

All that life offers belongs first to the industrious–

To those who build the plants and bake the bread.

When life and industry disconnect,

Where then are movements and leaders?

Where then inspiring culture and great achievement?

Treasure, good fortune, success, respect and civilization?

Those who would be wealthy work.

Success has a predictable footprint.

Initiative prompts and promotes,

Work prepares and performs.

Industry is prosperity and hope.

Indolence is poverty and despair.

Industry:

Harvests the crops,

Treats the patients,

Teaches the students,

Serves the customers,

And manufactures everything.

Work is the building block of virtue.

It is the magic pill that cures depression.

It is healing therapy for the resilient soul.

The workplace is as often the eye of the storm as it is a temple of reason and a place of peace.

Well-intended employers strive to create a happy shop.

Well-intended workers contribute to their success.

Employers:

Be good citizens.

Reward principled performance.

Value those who do the work and protect their entitlements.

Provide incentives.

A happy shop is safe.

Recognize ingenuity.

And share the wealth.

Workers:

Let your effort speak for you.

Industry is a powerful muscle; exercise it every day.

Employers:

Respect those who faithfully serve you.

Workers:

Respect those who faithfully lead you.

Lead and serve together in joy.

ACRIFICE

"When shall civilization be safe?" The mother of a soldier inquired.

Remember the soldiers' motto:

"No mission too difficult."

"No sacrifice too great."

"Duty first."

Whether you lay down your life for others,

As brave soldiers sometimes do,

Or act in the interest of others,

As everyone should,

Sacrifice is sacred.

When society is corrupted, values are ignored.

When citizens prefer comfort to principles,

Much that ought be valued is lost.

There are cycles of sin and repentance.

There are times of decline and renewal.

Embrace renewal.

If history teaches you nothing else, may it teach you this:

Sin and corruption produce misery and despair.

Reject decline.

When saints follow, when sinners lead, civilization self destructs.

When the perception is that the line between good and evil is blurred,

That right and wrong are shades of gray,

That morality is unimportant,

And sacrifice is obsolete,

Expect decline.

When decadence rules, who will be secure?

When shall civilization be safe?

"When no mission is too difficult."

"When no sacrifice is too great."

"When duty is first."

ERVICE

"Where is Peace?" Born poor but married well, the woman had acquired much and shared but little.

Consider the compulsive squirrel hoarding acorns for winter,

Unmindful of the clever fox who will catch her napping.

What value have acorns then?

Your agenda is yours to control,

But the season of your service is not.

Give yourself to something great while you can.

Peace draws strength from service.

You may take limited pleasure in late service, for it is better that you should serve than not.

You may be happy with the things that you acquire, for who doesn't like things?

But God forbid that you should fail to serve and never find your peace.

Some deign to serve only after they have first dazzled others with breathtaking possessions.

Their service is a sour footnote to what is the greater search for something more important –

Creating lives of unending ease for themselves.

There are those who spend their fertile seasons in the pursuit of mindless comfort.

Their service?   An afterthought funded by their surplus.

Their pleasure precedes their service.

Others live to serve, surrendering much of what little they have,

Making every season one of service.

Be prompt.

For lest you decide to quickly proceed, the time may never be right.

Prepare your offer on an altar of your choosing.

Tend someone sick.

Find someone a job.

Teach someone to read.

Take someone to church.

Bless the lives of those you love.

Serve others and be added upon.

Blossom or wither.

RECEIVING

"Is it shameful to Receive?" The man was *unavoidably unemployed.*

Those who must receive because of their need are not somehow diminished.

Those who must give because of their abundance are not somehow elevated.

Man is not measured like oil or coal – by his reserves –

Nor is he defined by need or the lack of it.

You are more than your surplus and greater than your need.

Those who give are not superior to those who must receive.

For what do they give that they too have not first received?

Those who give are no less indebted than those whose needs they recognize and fill.

Who has not had needs that others filled?

Who that now would serve has not been served?

For all have been served.

And everyone has taken.

Needs preceded generosity.

If no one had needs, who would be generous?

Will there be no generosity, no one generous?

Will there be no charity, no one charitable?

How will saints be trained?

Needs represent opportunity to those prepared to fill them.

Recognizing needs – that is their work.

Meeting needs – that is their glory.

Would you deprive them this?

Think not of those with needs as beggars,

As persons somehow less than you.

How blessed are they who give in the face of their need,

Sharing with others their widow's mite,

Without thought of reward.

Life, nurture, education, training,

receiving

Treasure, principles, love, support –

Give.

Generously.

Ask nothing back.

RATITUDE

"Ask nothing back?" He was a generous donor, but his gifts were not invisible.

Gratitude is not a commitment to bondage,

If gifts are *quid pro quo,* consider them wages and tainted.

A gift is not an indenture, and a donor is not a feudal lord.

Gratitude is not the wrenching cry of dependency.

Gratitude is thanks for kindness and recognition for service.

It is not an admission of servitude or a pledge of future performance.

Gratitude rankles the proud.

It is not that they would be ungrateful –

It is that they would not be dependent.

Pride is easily mistaken for ingratitude.

Pride considers need an embarrassment.

Generosity considers need an opportunity.

Need to pride implies shame, failure, defeat and humiliation.

Pride tolerates charity because it is desperate.

As pride despises need, failure, shame, defeat, and humiliation,

As generosity recognizes needs and moves to address them,

Those charitable remind those desperate of their dependency.

The prideful reject assistance to their hurt.

Gifts to those who need them are conspicuous.

To acknowledge the grantor and appreciate the gift is to confess defeat.

In a kinder, gentler world, gratitude is greater than pride,

And more important than the fear of dependency.

Grantors:

Gifts with conditions are toxic.

Beneficiaries:

When generosity partners with gratitude,

Good intentions make generous gifts complete.

Receive in joy as you would give in joy if you could.

Receive in joy as you will give in joy when you can.

PERFECTION

"Will we ever achieve Perfection?" *The interlocutor was impatient.*

The Teacher's unexpected response challenged the questioner's utopian vision.

Who will ever be complete?

And why should anyone want to be?

What great purpose might perfection be said to serve?

If men and women were perfect, maintenance would take priority over enterprise.

Come to this: Perfection is the death of initiative.

perfection

If the faithful are perfected, what shall happen to risk?

Who will dare to venture then, or make mistakes?

Are those called and chosen transfigured?

Translated from life?

Made over in death?

Is this how heaven works?

Will some favored faithful few understand all mysteries?

Speak to everyone in tongues?

Exercise power perfectly?

Will they prioritize?

Recognize every need?

Identify differences and comfort one and all?

Will the faithful chosen few live perfectly principled lives?

Will they control every human emotion?

Resist every kind of temptation?

Cultivate every laudable virtue?

Will they do what perfect knowledge requires?

And what if they should fail in this?

Will everything then be well?

Will they be perfect then?

Have you taken stock of eternity?

Is there time enough for this?

Is eternity a place of peace and repose?

Will the favored few pass the time in neutral?

Shall no one aspire to ever do anything better?

Will there be no new and challenging worlds to conquer there?

No rugged mountains yet to climb?

No powerful new initiatives?

No stunning new ideas?

Is heaven golden paths in green fields?

Cool drinks in delicious shade?

Palm fronds and lassitude?

Will everyone have everything anyone needs?

Will no one have anything less?

Will good and faithful servants whose work was well and faithfully done grow indolent there?

Spend their capital ostentatiously?

Claim some great inheritance?

What is better than perfection?

Learning, energy, restlessness and industry.

Every battle demands complicated logistics.

Winning, although wonderfully well valued, is never enough.

Every great achievement is but a pale shadow of something better yet to come.

Say this of perfection: "You can't get there from here."

Think of it as a distant dream out of reach to everyone.

You will always be discouraged.

You will always make mistakes.

You will never know everything.

And there will always be risks.

ACCOUNTABILITY

"Are we Accountable; shall there be a reckoning?"

Will everything be revealed?

Will everyone be seen for what they are?

Will dark secrets be shouted from the housetops?

Or will the evil men and women do be forgotten and excused?

Think you to escape the wrath to come?

Or that there is no wrath to come?

Have you looked into the pit of hell?

Or do you believe there is no pit of hell?

Is it vengeful to recognize sin and hold offenders to account?

What may we expect if there is no consequence for crime?

If murderers and thieves are never punished?

And there is no judgment?

Would you purchase a home in a neighborhood knowing there are criminals there?

Would you expect to live with them in peace?

Trust the safety of your children?

Or feel secure yourselves?

But what of those who say there is no wrath to come?

Who have considered the pit of hell and are unafraid?

Who, countenancing no eternity, fear no accounting and expect no reparations?

How shall they live?

What towering principle shall beckon them to greatness?

What sweeping vision shall help them hold a steady course?

To honor and uphold the law?

To act in the interest of others?

To do the good that they can do?

Those who do not contemplate a grand accounting must find other reasons to be good neighbors.

Who shall recognize evil, identify and punish offenders and see to reparations?

There are many who say that there is a loving God in heaven who hates injustice.

DEATH

"How shall we face Death?"

Like Socrates –

Philosophically.

After first examining life.

"Crito, we owe a cock to Aesculapius. Pay it and do not neglect it."

Those were Socrates' words spoken after he had raised the cup to his lips and drank, walked until his legs were heavy and the poison had begun to take effect.

"That," said Crito, "shall be done; but see if you have anything else to say."

"To this question he made no reply . . . ."

Following that undistinguished utterance, soon did end,

"[O]f all those of his time whom we have known," the life of "the best and wisest and most righteous man."

In life and death are details,

Unfinished tasks duty requires.

Like the cock.

Be prepared,

Forgetting not your debts.

For dotting i's and crossing t's,

Shall you traverse the Great Divide.

Do what is essential,

Each day.

Leave nothing to chance.

Count your blessings,

Each day.

And offer thanks.

What is to fear of death?

If life is eternal, enter your peace.

And if it is not, enter your peace.

Meet Him who sent you here,

And those who left you here,

And so rejoice,

Or sleep forever,

In peace.

If life is not eternal,

You will never know,

For you will know nothing.

If there is no great reunion,

You will never know.

You will not remember those you love,

And they in death will not remember you.

Nor shall they miss you.

Nor shall you miss them.

For you shall remember nothing,

And they shall remember nothing.

And there shall be nothing.

"Wherefore rejoice, what conquest brings he home?"

How little does it matter.

"What tributaries follow him to Rome?"

It will never matter.

If, conversely, your existence here,

Whenever so carefully considered –

This body, this mind, these creations, places, friends and powers –

Is seen as an incredible miracle,

Why should you not believe?

"[A]fter I drink the poison I shall no longer be with you, but shall go away to the joys of the blessed . . . ."

So spoke the great philosopher in contemplation of his impending death.

As he prepared to drink the bitter cup, he had inquired,

"What do you say about pouring a libation to some deity from this cup? May I, or not?"

"Socrates," his attendant dutifully replied, "we prepare only as much as we think is enough."

"I understand," he did respond, "but I may and must pray to the gods that my departure hence be a fortunate one; so I offer this prayer, and may it be granted."

When he drained the cup his companions wailed aloud, and he chastened them, "What conduct is this, you strange men! I sent the women away . . . that they might not behave in this absurd way; for I have heard that it is best to die in silence."

"Keep quiet and be brave."

Pray to God that your own departure may be "a fortunate one."

Ask that you may have the sense to "keep quiet and be brave."

Face your destiny like the noble Socrates.

ETERNITY

"How shall it be in Heaven?"

The Teacher spoke to his great hope.

Heaven is a healing place.

Broken hearts are repaired.

Those estranged are reconciled.

People strive for consensus and clarity rules.

Mistakes are corrected there.

Sins are forgiven there.

Those lost are found.

Freedom is respected.

eternity

Those who must have it are safe.

Saints find congregations to share their views,

And join together in peace with people like them.

Virtue is prized.

Friends are loyal.

Everyone is valued.

Success is lovingly shared.

Honesty is not the exception.

No one is punished for telling the truth.

Disciples practice what they preach,

Anger is tamed, and issues are resolved.

People govern themselves and do more than anyone requires.

Heaven is a place for those who speak softly but accomplish much.

It is a place for those who do good things for the right reasons.

For those who didn't hate.

Heaven is home to those who chose the path of honor and did their duty quietly.

To those who freely gave of their substance, renounced acclaim, forgot rewards and were interested in everyone.

Intolerance is not on any agenda there.

Doubt does not meet with disrespect,

Knowledge is power, and truth is not despised.

In heaven, performance is more important than grace,

And progress never stops.

History

"What did you miss?"

The answer was remarkably cheerful.

The first performance of Shakespeare's Lear,

Sparta, Athens, Carthage, and Rome,

The oratory of Demosthenes,

The sculpting of David,

Colloquy with Caesar,

And the Sermon on the Mount.

"Who did you miss?"

Now the question was remarkably cheerful.

Socrates and Plato,

Machiavelli, Cleopatra, Alexander,

Beethoven, Voltaire and Catherine the Great.

Jefferson, Lincoln, the Duke of Wellington and Marshall Ney,

The Baptist, the Rock named Peter, the Apostle named Paul, the fallen Judas, and Christ.

History is humanity exposed.

Corrupt monarchs,

Scheming cardinals,

Seductive concubines,

Crusades and inquisitions,

Murdered princes and treacherous regents.

Heroes, champions, teachers, servants, scholars and saints.

History is capricious and fickle.

Master its lessons,

Many of them joyous.

Accept the blessed.

Reject the cursed.

Learn from both.

ELIEF

"What do you Believe?"

I believe in truth and freedom and in everyone else who does.

I believe truth and freedom are more important than uniformity of belief.

I believe those who promote the faith at the expense of the truth are deceivers.

I believe in republican principles.

That we should "speak softly and carry a big stick."

That "all that is necessary for the triumph of evil is for good men to do nothing."

I prefer reckless liberty to stultifying order.

I prefer the fringes of chaos to the Prussian army.

And my love of freedom is greater than my fear of death.

I reject conceit, incivility, class warfare, discrimination, genocide and demagogues.

I reject arrogance, exclusion, polarization, all manner of fraud and every kind of addiction.

I reject the breakdown of personal discipline, shallow ideals, bulldog disciples, unsavory shepherds, censors, apologists, friends of order and enemies of truth.

I believe in freedom of expression and thought, in honesty and open minds.

That we should live as we speak and do what we say we will.

I believe that good things follow extraordinary effort,

That decency is success,

That depravity is failure,

That faith is not the victory of feelings over facts,

And that we shall be surprised to see who sits down in the kingdom of heaven.

LESSONS

A respected student rose to say, "What have you learned, Teacher?"

He stood to his full height, awkward, but proud and straight.

I have learned that we are blessed in ways we least expect.

I have learned to trust myself,

To sift the wheat from the chaff,

That conclusions must follow findings of fact,

And that things are never quite what they seem to be.

I have learned that there are fewer absolutes than
I was led to believe,

That certainty is mother to many mistakes,

And that no one owns the truth.

I have learned that I am home at sea.

Finis

INIS

* * *

He had counseled them from the heart.

He had spoken directly, holding nothing back.

He had treated this mountain as a high and holy place,

And respected this convocation as a beloved assembly of saints and friends.

He had described the learning of a generous lifetime.

When he had finished, all was quiet.

By their silence they did think to honor him.

As he prepared to leave, they quietly rose until everyone stood.

There had been a feeling there.

He had not created a movement or claimed divinity.

He had made lasting impressions in simple ways in quiet places.

* * *

The rock church could not accommodate those who came to honor him,

Those who had become inadvertent stewards of his legacy.

As witnesses to his extraordinary life, they had quoted him.

Through their remembrance his fame had spread.

As loosely tethered and accidental disciples they had nurtured him.

They had offered him privacy and peace, and he had tutored them.

Many had come from great distances to this place.

Some of them who came had everything; others nothing at all.

He had spoken to their different hearts to like effect.

And he had never let them down.

A few of the visitors asked the elders for permission to speak of him.

They spoke of his wit and of his wisdom and of his passion.

The procession was long and unusually solemn. It wound its way from the tiny stone church past the edge of the small village to the base of a rolling hill. Here would the Teacher be at rest.

When they had finished their tributes, traveled to his chosen place of last repose and seen him lowered into the earth, they spoke yet again:

"Lord look with favor upon our friend. Bless this extraordinary man and protect this peaceful place."

When they left they remembered what he said to them . . . . *"I am home at sea."*

"Peace is not a seamless web."

Men fear thought as they fear nothing else on earth – more than ruin, more even than death. Thought is subversive and revolutionary, destructive and terrible; thought is merciless to privilege, established institutions, and comfortable habits; thought is anarchic and lawless, indifferent to authority, careless of the well-tried wisdom of the ages. Thought looks into the pit of hell and is not afraid. It sees man, a feeble speck, surrounded by unfathomable depths of silence; yet it bears itself proudly, as unmoved as if it were lord of the universe. Thought is great and swift and free, the light of the world, and the chief glory of man.

Bertrand Russell